Splat the Cat
Doodle & Draw
A Coloring & Activity Book

W9-BEP-390

Based on the bestselling
books by Rob Scotton

Text by Emily C. Hughes

Illustrations by Rick Farley

HARPER FESTIVAL
An Imprint of HarperCollinsPublishers

HarperFestival is an imprint of HarperCollins Publishers.
Copyright © 2013 by Rob Scotton
All rights reserved. Manufactured in China.
No part of this book may be used or reproduced in any manner whatsoever without written permission except in the case of brief quotations embodied in critical articles and reviews.
For information address HarperCollins Children's Books, a division of HarperCollins Publishers, 10 East 53rd Street, New York, NY 10022.
www.harpercollinschildrens.com
ISBN 978-0-06-211607-9
Typography by Rick Farley
12 13 14 15 16   SCP   10 9 8 7 6 5 4 3 2 1
❖
First Edition

This is Splat! Can you color in his fur?

This is Splat with his pet mouse, Seymour.

Draw a picture of your pet!

These are Splat's parents. Finish drawing his family.

This is Splat's sister and Splat's brother.

What would your family look like as cats? Draw them!

Splat and Seymour love to ride on Splat's bike.
What are they riding past?

Copy this picture of Splat riding his bike.

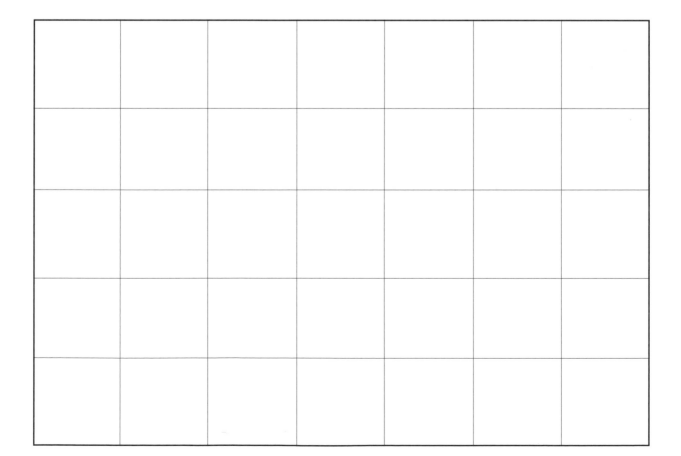

Design Splat and Seymour's new bike helmets!

Splat is trying to ride his bike to school—help him get there!

START

FINISH

Answer key on page 64.

Draw a picture of your school.

These are some of Splat's favorite things. Color the ones you like, too!

Draw some of your favorite things!

Splat goes to Cat School with his friends.
Draw more cats and color everyone in!

Mrs. Wimpydimple is teaching the class.
Draw her lesson on the blackboard.

Splat's best friends are Spike, Plank, and Kitten.
Color in their fur and clothes.

Draw some of your friends!

Spike and Splat are playing with Splat's toys.
Draw Spike juggling your favorite toy!

Uh-oh! Spike accidentally broke some of Splat's stuff.
Can you put his things back together?
Draw a line between the matching pieces.

It's Valentine's Day, and Splat made a valentine for Kitten!
Draw it.

Five things are different about Kitten in these two pictures.
Can you find and circle them?

Answer key on page 64.

Splat's favorite snack is candy fish.
Draw more fish to fill his bag!

One of these pictures of Splat is different from the others.
Circle the one that's different!

Answer key on page 64.

Splat is making a jack-o'-lantern.
What kind of face does it have?

Splat needs your help deciding on a Halloween costume!
What should he be?

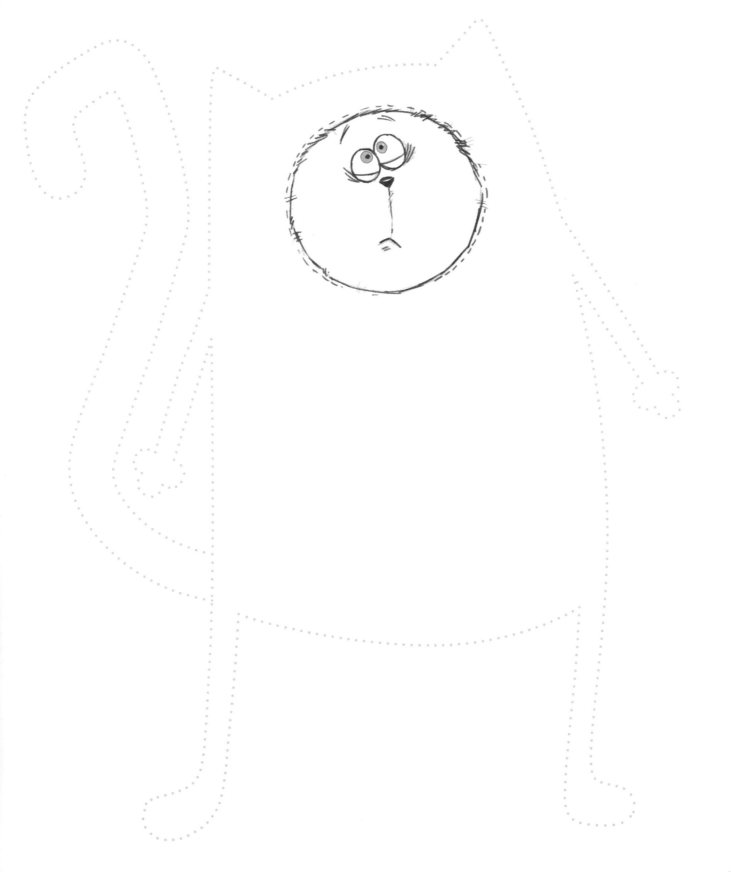

Seymour made Splat some cupcakes.
How many cupcakes do you count?

Design your own cupcake.

Spike, Splat, and Plank are camping out.

Oh, no! Splat is scared.
Draw a spooky shadow on the wall of the tent!

Splat is helping his mom decorate the Christmas tree!
Can you draw the decorations?

Help Splat and his sister build a snowman!

What was the best present you ever got? Draw it!

Splat's dad makes ducks. How many ducks do you count?

Design your own duck.

Splat's class is learning to swim.
What does Splat's new bathing suit look like?

Draw Splat and his friends in the pool!

Splat's favorite TV show is *Super Cat!*
Show Super Cat keeping the streets safe.

Help Splat get dressed up in Super Cat's costume!

Splat is baking a cake. What ingredients will he need?

Draw Splat's cake!

Now Splat has to clean up.
Draw Splat making suds!

Uh-oh—Seymour is caught in a big bubble. Draw him!

Splat is excited to go to Cat School.
What does Splat's face look like when he's happy?

What do you look like when you're happy?

Splat's class is going on a field trip.
Draw Splat and his friends inside the bus!

Spike also has a pet mouse. Can you decorate his mouse hole?

Splat found a duck who needs glasses.
Will you draw him a pair?

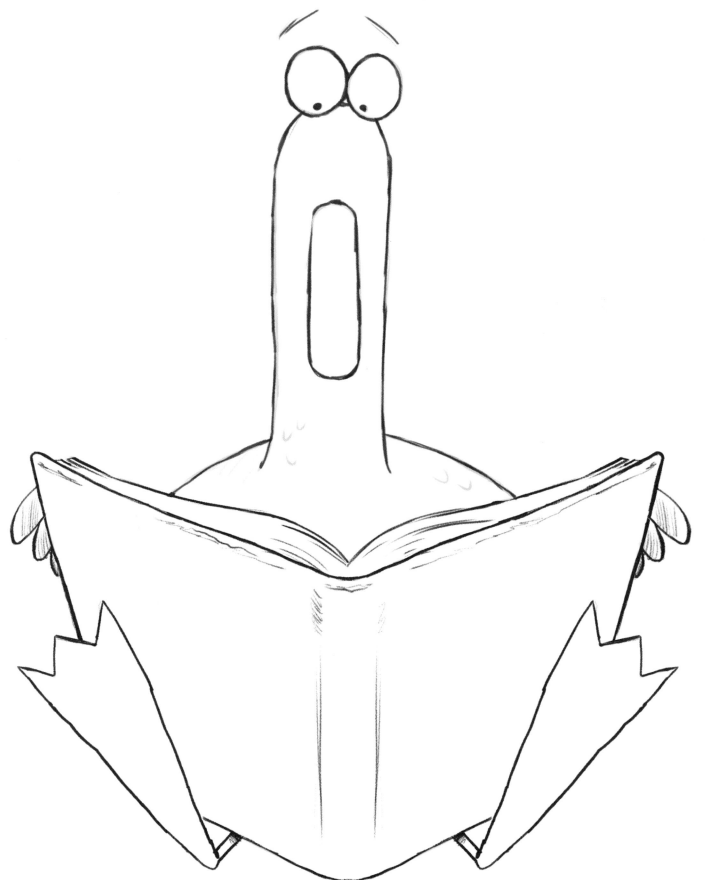

It's raining and Splat can't go skating—what a pain!

Copy the drawing from the opposite page here.

Splat and Seymour are pretending to be pirates!
Draw them on their ship.

Draw Cap'n Splat's treasure map!

Now Splat is pretending to be an astronaut.
Can you draw him in a spacesuit?

Draw Splat and decorate his rocket ship!

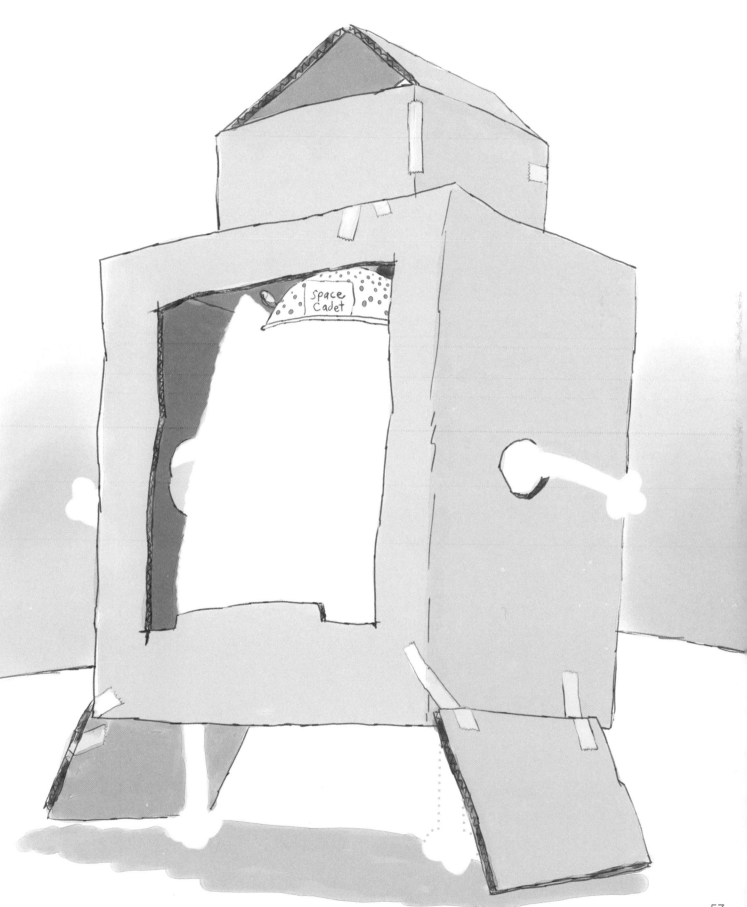

space
Cadet

Splat doesn't like to take baths—the water is too scary and too wet.
Can you help Splat get in the bath by drawing him?

Do you like baths? Draw some things that you use to take a bath.

Here is Splat's drawing of Seymour.
Draw a picture of your favorite animal!

Seymour

What is Seymour thinking about?

Help Spike and Plank find their way to Splat's den.

START

FINISH

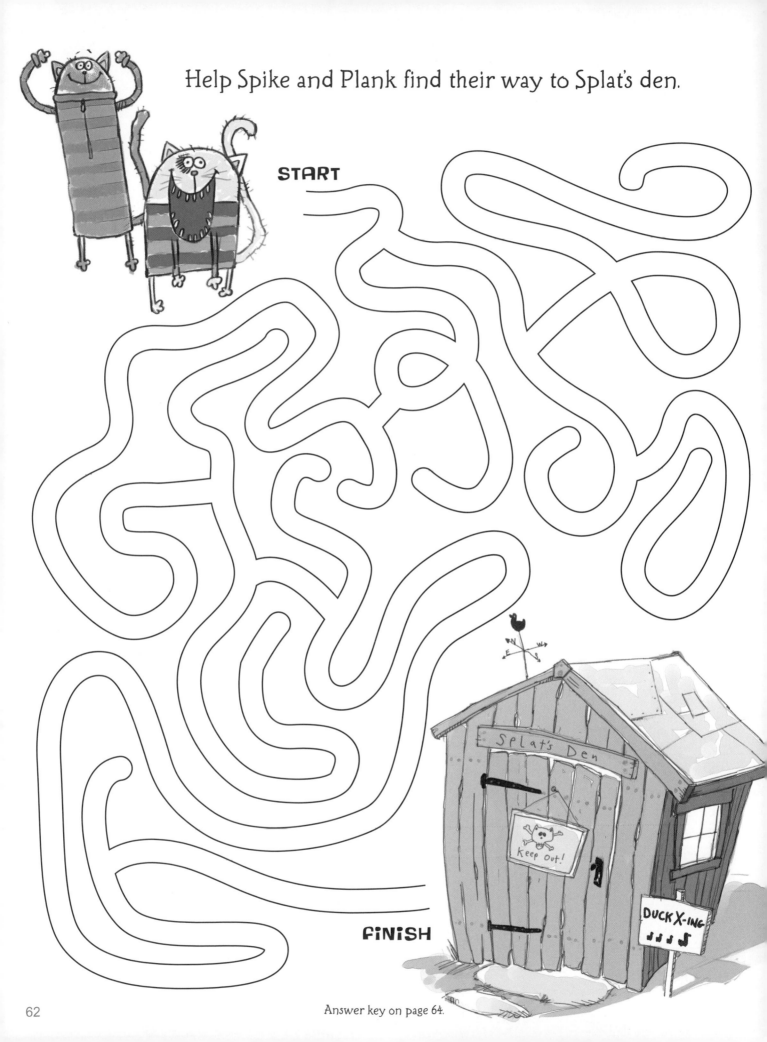

Keep Out!

Splat's Den

DUCK X-ING

Answer key on page 64.

Draw yourself with Splat and Seymour!

ANSWER KEY

Page 12

Splat is trying to ride his bike to school—help him get there!

Page 21

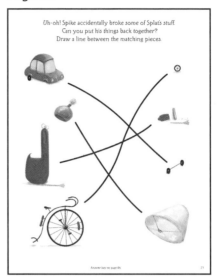

Uh-oh! Spike accidentally broke some of Splat's stuff.
Can you put his things back together?
Draw a line between the matching pieces.

Page 23

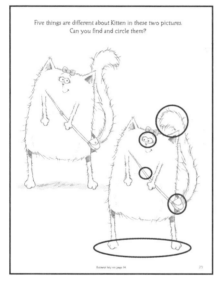

Five things are different about Kitten in these two pictures.
Can you find and circle them?

Page 25

One of these pictures of Splat is different from the others.
Circle the one that's different!

Page 62

Help Spike and Plank find their way to Splat's den.